Trains

By
Margaret Snyder

Illustrated by
Mary Teichman

© 1999 McClanahan Book Company, Inc.
All rights reserved.
Published by McClanahan Book Company, Inc.
23 West 26th Street, New York, NY 10010
ISBN: 0-7681-0135-2
Printed in the U.S.A.
10 9 8 7 6 5 4 3 2 1

Chug-chug-chug! *Choo-choo*! The train rounded the corner and then pulled slowly into the station. The brakes hissed as it came to a stop.

Robby watched the big train from the platform. He was very excited. He was about to take his very first train ride ever!

"All aboard!" The conductor called to all the waiting passengers. They bustled to form a straight line.

"I'm going to visit my grandpa," Robby said as he handed his ticket to the conductor.

"I hope you have a good trip," the conductor told Robby as he punched the ticket. *Click-click*.

There were many open seats in the train car. Robby picked one next to the window. He didn't want to miss seeing anything!

In a few minutes, the train whistle blew. *Toot-toot*!
And the train lurched forward. *Cha-chunk*!
They were on their way!

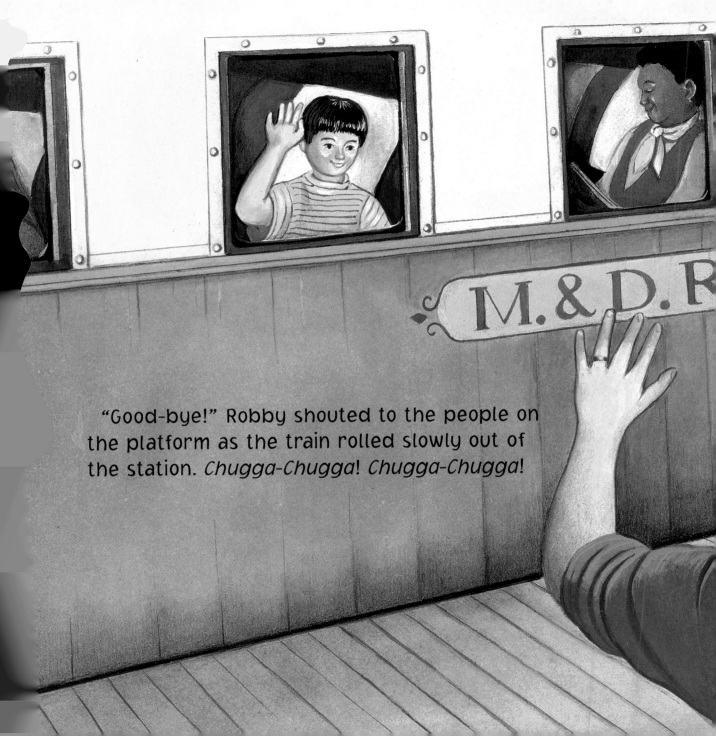

"Good-bye!" Robby shouted to the people on the platform as the train rolled slowly out of the station. *Chugga-Chugga! Chugga-Chugga!*

The people on the platform waved back at him. Their journeys were over, but Robby's was just beginning!

Clickety-Clack! *Clickety-Clack*! The train picked up speed. The station was soon just a dot in the distance as the train made its way out of the city. Robby couldn't take his eyes off the blur of office buildings, streets, and houses.

Suddenly, he heard a new sound—*Ding! Ding! Ding!*—and saw two red flashing lights. Cars were stopped at a railroad crossing, waiting for the train to pass.

Just then the door to Robby's car opened. *Ting-a-ling! Ting-a-ling!* A chef walked into the car ringing a dinner bell. "Dinner is now served!" he announced.

"Whoa!" Robby cried as he stood up. The train cars rocked from side to side, and Robby lost his balance.

"Hang onto those seat rails," the chef said.

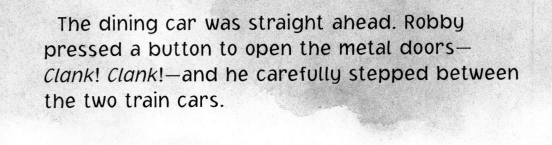

The dining car was straight ahead. Robby
pressed a button to open the metal doors—
Clank! *Clank*!—and he carefully stepped between
the two train cars.

Menu
M & D R R
CRAB BISQUE
COCONUT SOUP
CORN CAKES
W/ GOAT CHEESE
LEMON CHICKEN
LOBSTER TAC
SMOKED TUR
SALAD
PENNE W/S
CREME D
LEMON

"Wow!" Robby said. "I can see everything."
The dining car had big windows all the way
around it! Outside the train, the countryside
was whizzing past.

From the dining car, Robby could also see the big, black engine pulling the train. The powerful engine's shiny wheels turned round and round, pulling all the other cars.

Robby knew what he wanted to be when he grew up—a train engineer! He would drive the train and blow the whistle to let people know that the train was coming. *Toot! Toot!*

Clickety-clack! *Clickety-clack*! The train swayed
as it went around a bend, and the caboose at
the back came into view.

"Can I ride in it?" he asked one
of the conductors.

"The caboose is an office for the people who work on the train," the conductor said. "But I can let you take a quick look. Come on, let's go."
"Thanks!" Robby said.

Just then, Robby heard a faint whistle.
Woo-woo! A freight train was approaching on
the sidetrack.

Tanker cars filled with oil, timber stacked on flatbed cars, and rack cars filled with automobiles rushed by making Robby's train tremble. Within seconds the fast freight train was gone . . .

WHOOSH!

Later that evening, Robby went to one of the
train's sleeping cars. There were two bunks.
"Top bunk!" he yelled.

Robby put on his pajamas and hopped into bed. It had been a very busy day, and the gentle motion of the train now made him very sleepy.

Robby dreamed of telling his grandpa all about his trip. And as Robby dreamed, the train kept rolling quietly through the starry night. *Clickety-clack! Clickety-clack! Clickety-clack!*